A WILD ADVENTURE

Illustrations by Alan Batson & Grace Mills
Cover design by Megan McLaughlin. Cover illustration by Alan Batson & Grace Mills.

Little, Brown and Company
Hachette Book Group
1290 Avenue of the Americas, New York, NY 10104

Visit us at LBYR.com

First Edition: August 2021

Little, Brown and Company is a division of Hachette Book Group, Inc. The Little, Brown name and logo are trademarks of Hachette Book Group, Inc.

The publisher is not responsible for websites (or their content) that are not owned by the publisher.

Library of Congress Control Number: 2021938403

ISBNs: 978-0-316-62811-2 (paper over board), 978-0-316-62814-3 (ebook), 978-0-316-62810-5 (ebook), 978-0-316-62812-9 (ebook)

PRINTED IN THE UNITED STATES OF AMERICA

PHX

10 9 8 7 6 5 4 3 2 1

DREAMWORKS

Spirit

A WILD ADVENTURE

Adapted by **MEREDITH RUSU**

Illustrated by **ALAN BATSON** & **GRACE MILLS**

Little, Brown and Company
New York Boston

Have you ever been someplace new that's so big and open and *wild*, it makes you feel nervous and excited at the same time?

That's how I felt when I first moved to Miradero. My name is Lucky, by the way. And this is my home.

It was scary moving out to the frontier at first.
I wasn't sure I would fit in very well.

But sometimes, being in a new place can bring out
the wild side in you, too! My friends taught me that.

Speaking of friends, these are mine: Abigail and Pru. They know everything about frontier life!

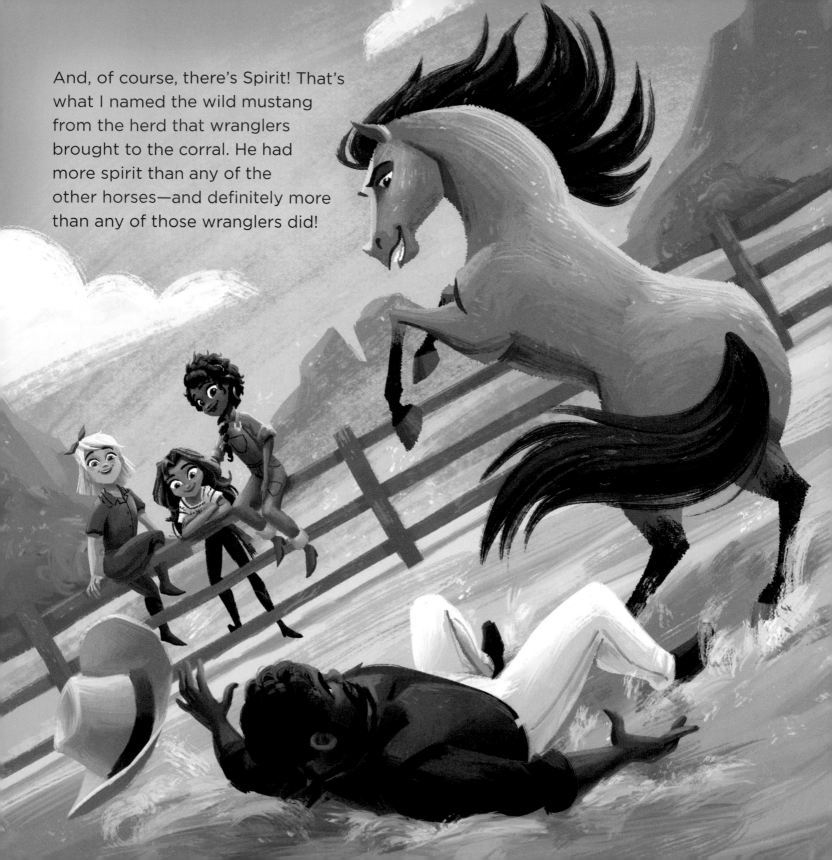

And, of course, there's Spirit! That's what I named the wild mustang from the herd that wranglers brought to the corral. He had more spirit than any of the other horses—and definitely more than any of those wranglers did!

Spirit wasn't sure what to think of me at first. It can be hard to trust new people, especially when you're in a strange new place.

But Pru and Abigail taught me that these things take time. True friendship is built bit by bit. Memory by memory. And sometimes, apple by apple.

By the time Spirit and I became friends, a wrangler named Hendricks and his crew had captured Spirit's entire herd. They were going to ship off the horses and sell them all over the world. Spirit's herd would never be free again!

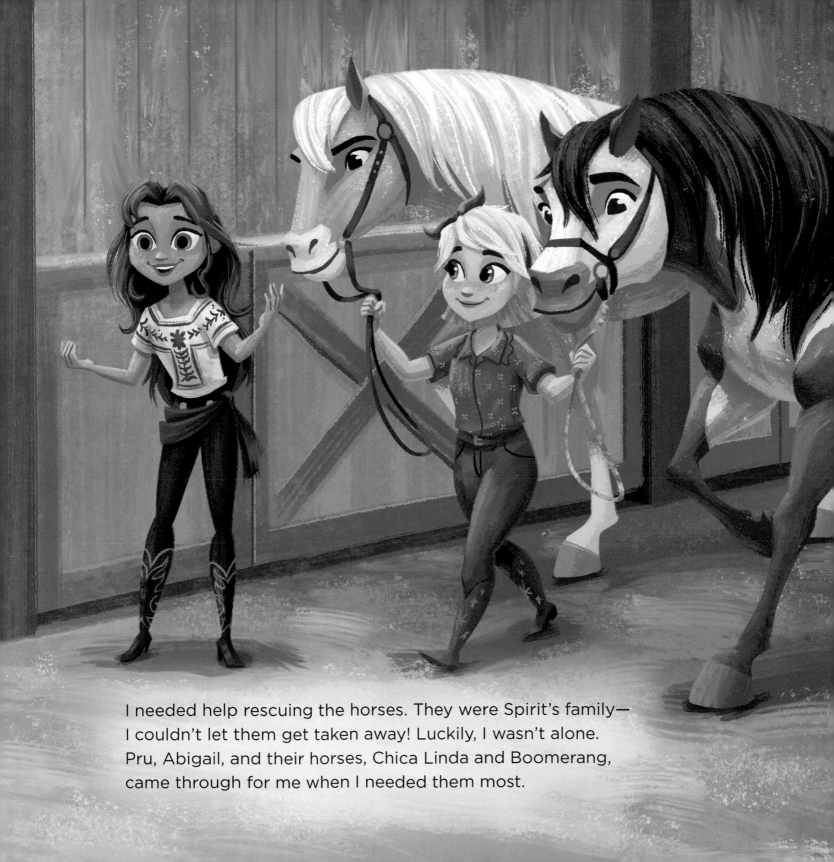

I needed help rescuing the horses. They were Spirit's family—
I couldn't let them get taken away! Luckily, I wasn't alone.
Pru, Abigail, and their horses, Chica Linda and Boomerang,
came through for me when I needed them most.

It was going to be a dangerous mission. We had to stop the wranglers from loading Spirit's herd onto a cargo ship. But reaching them in time meant taking a shortcut across a wide ravine and climbing over a steep mountain.

Our journey got off to a rocky start. And I started feeling pretty worried.

Pru and Abigail had lived here all their lives and knew how to handle tough terrain. But would I?

Spirit could tell I was jittery, and that only made things worse.

But then Pru and Abigail taught me the most important horsemanship lesson of all: "When you trust yourself, your horse will trust you, too."

My friends were right. I may not have lived in Miradero my whole life, but I could still pull myself back up and dust myself off.

I could be strong and brave
and let courage lead the way.

And I could believe in myself, just like my friends believed in me.

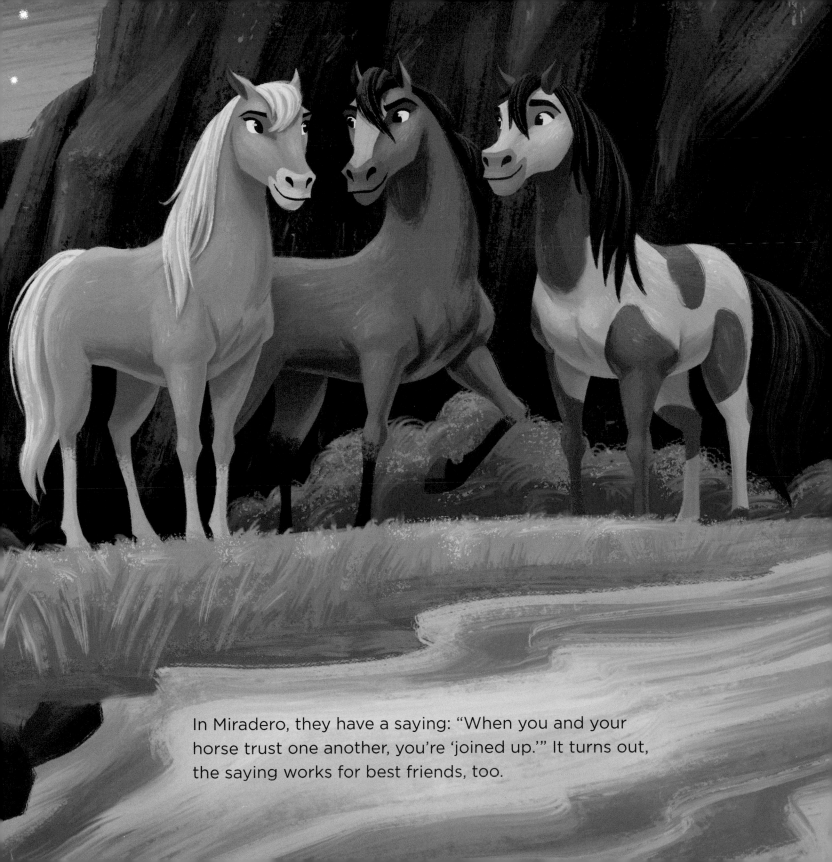

In Miradero, they have a saying: "When you and your horse trust one another, you're 'joined up.'" It turns out, the saying works for best friends, too.

I didn't realize it at the time, but my adventure wasn't just about finding Spirit's herd...

it was about finding the courage
to let my own wild spirit shine.

Working together, Pru, Abigail, and I got to the horses just in time and rounded up the wranglers. We had saved Spirit's herd!

We were so happy. Soon, all the horses were running free again.

Even though I knew letting Spirit return to the wild meant I might never see him again, I had to let him be true to himself, too.

Besides, I had a feeling that with best friends like Abigail and Pru, there were still lots of wild adventures to come.